# Minnie and Moo
# Go to the Moon

## Denys
## Cazet

SCHOLASTIC INC.
New York   Toronto   London   Auckland   Sydney
Mexico City   New Delhi   Hong Kong

## for Liza Russ, a friend

*A Richard Jackson Book*

ISBN 0-439-08189-0

Published by Scholastic Inc., 555 Broadway, New York, NY 10012, by arrangement with DK, Inc., an imprint of DK Publishing, Inc., New York. All rights reserved. SCHOLASTIC and associated logos are trademarks and/or registered trademarks of Scholastic Inc.

12 11 10 9 8 7 6 5 4 3 2 1     9/9 0 1 2 3 4/0

Printed in the U.S.A.        24

First Scholastic printing, February 1999

The illustrations for this book were created with pencil and watercolor. The illustration on these pages was drawn in pencil. The text of this book was set in 18 point Berling.

# Moo Thinks

The farmer stopped the tractor.

He dusted himself off

and walked to the farmhouse.

He stopped at the screen door

and took off his boots.

He hung up his hat on an old nail

and went into the house.

Moo looked at Minnie.

She pointed at the tractor.

She pointed at the hay baler.

"We could do that," she said.

Minnie took the straw
out of her mouth.
"Do what?" she asked.
"Drive that tractor," said Moo.

"Oh, Moo, Moo," said Minnie.

"You have been thinking again."

"It was only a small think," said Moo.

Minnie put her arm around Moo.

"Moo," she said. "We are cows.

Cows give milk.

It is what we do.

The farmer cannot give milk.

That is why farmers drive tractors

and cows do not."

"No," said Moo.

"I have been thinking.

What does the farmer have

that we do not?"

"Hands and feet," said Minnie.

"No," said Moo. "Boots and a hat!"

# Moo Explains

"Boots and a hat?" said Minnie.

"Yes," said Moo. "Boots and a hat.

When the farmer is outside,

he puts on his boots and his hat.

Then he drives the tractor.

When he goes inside, he takes off

his boots and hangs his hat on a nail.

He does not drive the tractor.

He cannot drive the tractor

without his hat or his boots," said Moo.

"But Moo . . ." said Minnie.

"Think!" said Moo, tapping her head.

"Use your brain.

Have you ever seen the farmer

drive the tractor in his house?"

"No," said Minnie. "But . . ."

"See," said Moo. "He cannot drive

the tractor without boots and a hat!"

"Moo!" said Minnie.

"We do not have boots.

We do not have a hat.

We cannot drive the tractor!"

Moo looked at the farmer's porch.

She looked at the boots.

She looked at the hat
hanging on a nail.

She looked at Minnie and smiled.

"I get to wear the hat," said Minnie.

# The Magic Words

Moo put on the farmer's boots.

She climbed onto the tractor.

"Ready?" she shouted.

Minnie put on the farmer's hat.

"Ready!" she yelled.

Moo moved a lever.

She stepped on the gas.

The tractor didn't move.

Moo pulled a handle.

She stepped on a pedal.

The tractor was quiet.

"Try the magic words," said Moo.
"The ones the farmer shouts
when the tractor won't start."
"Okay," said Minnie.

"YOU CHEESY PIECE OF JUNK!
YOU BROKEN-DOWN, NO-GOOD,
RUSTY BUCKET OF BOLTS!"

Moo turned the key.

The tractor grumbled.

"Try it again," shouted Moo.

"This time, kick the tires

*after* you say the magic words."

Moo turned the key again.

Minnie shouted,

"YOU CHEESY PIECE OF JUNK!

YOU BROKEN-DOWN, NO-GOOD,

RUSTY BUCKET OF BOLTS!"

She kicked the tires.

*Roooaarrr!* went the tractor.

*Whooosh!* went the hay baler.

# Flight

Minnie jumped back on the tractor.

"Look at that," she shouted.

Hay bales rolled out behind them.

"I'm so proud," said Moo.

"I could sing.

   *"The hills are alive,*

   *with the sound of moo-sic . . ."*

Suddenly

the tractor crashed into the pigsty.

Mud flew up.

Pigs grunted.

"Duck!" Minnie shouted.

A pig whizzed by.

"That was no duck!" shouted Moo.

"Slow down," yelled Minnie.

"I can't," yelled Moo.

"We're going faster!"

Clouds of dust filled the sky.

The tractor crashed
into the chicken coop.
Eggs rained down.

Chickens flew into the hay baler.

The tractor went faster and faster.

It roared through the hay field.

It roared over the hill.

It roared into the air.

"We're flying!" shouted Moo.

"We're in outer space!"

shouted Minnie.

# On the Moon

*Crash!* went the tractor.

*Bash!* went the hay baler.

They spun around and around.

Dust and rocks flew everywhere.

Then they stopped.

It was quiet.

"Where are we?" asked Moo.

Minnie waved the dust away.

She looked at all the rocks.

She looked at the big hole.

they were sitting in.

"I knew it," said Minnie.

"We are on the moon!"

"The moon?" said Moo.

Moo stepped off the tractor.

"This does not look like the moon.

The moon is made of cheese," she said.

Minnie walked over to Moo.

"Moo," she said. "Look around you.

What do you see?"

"I see a big hole.

I see the farmer's tractor.

I see the hay baler.

They are sitting at the bottom

of a big hole," said Moo.

"Crater!" said Minnie.

"On the moon, a hole is a 'crater.'"

"Look!" said Moo. "Snow!"

Feathers drifted down from the sky.

"The moon is very cold," said Minnie.

"It does not feel cold," said Moo.

"The moon is a very strange place."

"It is," said Minnie. "Look over there!

There are some moonsters!"

# Attack
# of the Moonsters

Six chickens stared at Minnie and Moo.

Their feathers were gone.

They were mad.

"They look like chickens," said Moo.

"Don't be silly," said Minnie.

"There are no chickens on the moon.

Moo, don't you understand?

Didn't you know?

There is no air on the moon.

Chickens need air to breathe.

Use your brain," she said,

tapping her head.

"These are moonsters, not chickens.

Chickens have feathers."

"Minnie," said Moo.

"I have been thinking. . . .

If there is no air,

how can we—"

Suddenly the chickens

pecked at Minnie and Moo!

"Ouch!" cried Minnie.

Minnie jumped up and down.

"Ouch! Ouch! Ouch!"

"Run, Minnie," shouted Moo.

"Ouch! Ouch! Ouch!"

37

"Start the tractor," yelled Minnie.

"Say the magic words!" shouted Moo.

"YOU CHEESY PIECE OF—ouch—
JUNK—ouch! YOU RUSTY—ouch—
BUCKET OF—ouch, ouch—BOLTS!
YOU BROKEN-DOWN,
NO-GOOD—ouch, ouch!

"Hurry, Moo!" cried Minnie.

"Kick the tires!" shouted Moo.

"Turn the key!" shouted Minnie.

*Roooaarrr!* went the tractor.

*Whoooosh!* went the hay baler.

The tractor shot up the crater and flew into the air.

# Home Again

*SPLOOSH!*

The tractor landed in the duck pond.

The hay baler groaned.

The tractor moaned.

It hissed a cloud of steam.

Minnie and Moo

climbed out of the pond.

They looked back at the tractor.

The farmer's hat

and one of his boots

floated on the water.

"Oh-oh," said Moo.

"Here comes the farmer,"

"Run!" said Minnie.

Minnie and Moo

jumped over the fence.

"Quick," said Moo. "Get down!"

"Eat some grass!" said Minnie.

The farmer walked to the pond.

He looked at his tractor.

He looked at his hay baler.

He looked at the holes in his hat.

He picked up his boot
and poured water out of it.

The farmer saw two cows eating grass.

"Is he still looking at us?" asked Moo.

"I think he's looking at you,"

said Minnie.

"Me?" said Moo. "Why me?"

"You're wearing his other boot,"

said Minnie.

"Oh-oh!" said Moo.